Tots and the Hedgehog

Written by Ragdoll

Illustrated by Penny Lane

A Ragdoll Production for Central Independent Television

Scholastic Children's Books,
Scholastic Publications Ltd,
7-9 Pratt Street, London NW1 0AE

Scholastic Inc.,
730 Broadway, New York, NY 10003, USA

Scholastic Canada Ltd,
123 Newkirk Road, Richmond Hill,
Ontario, Canada L4C 3G5

Ashton Scholastic Pty Ltd,
PO Box 579, Gosford, New South Wales,
Australia

Ashton Scholastic Ltd,
Private Bag 1, Penrose, Auckland,
New Zealand

Published by Scholastic Children's Books 1993

Original script Robin Stevens, Anne Wood, Andrew Davenport.
Text adapted by Jack Ousbey

ISBN 0 590 55484 0

Typeset by Rapid Reprographics
Printed in Great Britain by Bath Press Colourbooks, Glasgow

All was quiet in the secret house where the Tots lived. Tilly woke up first.

"Bonjour Tots," she said.

"Good morning, Tilly," said Tiny.

"Tots," said Tom, "I think something interesting is going to happen today. I have a feeling, I have."

Tiny took the magic bag from its peg and they were ready to go adventuring out.

"Ee-aw," said Donkey as they went through the garden.

"What will we see today?" sang the Tots. "What will we see?"

"Peek a boo," said Furryboo.

At the edge of the woods the Tots stopped.

"Regarde," said Tilly.
"Yes, look," said Tiny. "There's something hiding under there."

Prickle coat hedgehog
see how he goes,
Sniffling the ground
with his snuffly nose.
Nobody seems to
bother him much,
Please don't touch.

Very carefully, Tom cleared away some of the leaves.

"See Tots," he said. "It's a hedgehog. Hedgehogs
often curl up and go to sleep like that."

"But it's nearly the middle of the day," said Tiny in
a loud voice.

7

"Shhh," said Tom. "You'll wake him up. Hedgehogs
go to sleep in the day, they do, and wake up at night."
"Ah, bien," said Tilly, "une bonne idée."

Just then the Tots heard voices. Two men with brooms were sweeping the path and coming towards them.

"Oh dear," said Tiny, "those sweepers are going to sweep up hedgehog."

"He's frightened," said Tom. "He's curling himself up into a ball. Hedgehogs do that when they're frightened, you know."

But Tilly knew how to help. She took out her magic flute and began to play. Hedgehog wasn't frightened any more. He uncurled himself and scuttled away just in time. As he went to look for a new hiding place, Tom and Tiny joined in with Tilly's tune -

Prickle coat hedgehog
see how he goes,
Sniffling the ground
with his snuffly nose.
Nobody seems to
bother him much,
Please don't touch.

"That's better," thought Tilly. "He can go back to sleep now all safe and sound."

The Tots set off for home, pleased that they had been able to help hedgehog.

"You're a good singer, Tom," said Tiny. "You sang the hedgehog song very well."

"I am quite a good singer of songs," said Tom, "I enjoy a little sing-song."

"Shall we sing another song?" said Tiny. "Shall we sing The Going Back Home Song?"

And they began.

What a lovely morning,
Let's all give a shout,
We are coming home again,
We've been adventuring out.
We've seen a spiky hedgehog
We've sung a hedgehog song.
Exploring done, here we come,
Back home where we belong.

Tilly didn't sing. She was too busy thinking what fun
it would be if she were a hedgehog and could sleep
during the day.

When they got home, Tilly and Tiny went upstairs and
all was quiet. Tom found his book and settled down
to read. He had only read a page or two when he
heard Tilly and Tiny giggling and whispering
upstairs.

"Do be quiet, Tots," he shouted. "I am trying to read,
I am."

Just then, Tiny appeared at the top of the stairs.
  "Guess what Tilly's doing, Tom," said Tiny.
  "What?" asked Tom.
  "Listen," said Tiny.

They heard bumping, thumping sounds, and then
Tilly's voice.

"Un, deux, trois," – THUMP! "Un, deux, trois," –
THUMP!

"What is Tilly doing?" asked Tom. "One, two,
three, thumping about."

"You'll see," said Tiny and went off to feed
Donkey.

Tom had just started to
read again when a big,
floppy mattress came
flip, flop, flapping
down the stairs,
followed by a fat,
fluffy pillow.

"What are you ..." Tom started to call when a huge blanket billowed through the air, floated down and covered him from head to toe.

"Tilly," spluttered Tom, pulling at the blanket. "What is going on please?"

"Bonjour, Tom," said Tilly. She was standing on the stairs, dressed in her pyjamas and carrying her teddy bear. Tom pointed at the mattress.

"Is that what I think it is, that came flip-flopping down the stairs?"

"Oui," said Tilly. "C'est mon lit."

"I can see it's your bed, Tilly," cried Tom. "But why is it downstairs? Somebody might trip over it."

And just then, somebody did. Tiny came back from
feeding Donkey and fell over the pillow and on to the
mattress. But Tilly didn't notice. She was drawing
the curtains. She wanted to shut out the daylight so
that she could have a daytime sleep – like hedgehog.

Tilly made her bed and then snuggled under the blanket.

"Bonne nuit, Tiny. Bonne nuit, Tom."

"Goodnight," they said.

"Bonne nuit," whispered Tilly and fell fast asleep.

Tom looked at Tiny and said –

Naughty Tilly's moved her bed,
Moved her bed, moved her bed.
Naughty Tilly's moved her bed,
She wants to sleep in the daytime.

Tom and Tiny giggled. Then Tiny whispered back –

Tilly's curled up nice and warm,
Nice and warm, nice and warm.
Tilly's curled up nice and warm,
She thinks that she's a hedgehog.

It was dark in the house with the curtains drawn. Tom couldn't see to read his book.

"I can't even see to read," said Tom. "I am very, very bored."

"And I am extremely bored," said Tiny, stamping his foot.

Tilly woke up. "Shhh," she said.

"This is silly," said Tom. "Let's go outside."

It wasn't much better outside in the garden. They played on the swing but soon got bored; they played on the cart and that was boring too. Just then, Tom caught sight of Donkey looking over his stable door.

"Donkey looks as though he needs an apple," said Tom.

"But the apples are in the house where Tilly's asleep," said Tiny.

"I know," said Tom, "but if I need a nice apple for
Donkey I'll have to go inside, won't I?"

So Tom crept carefully into the house on tiptoe. Quiet as he was, he almost woke Tilly as he took an apple from the basket. And now it was Tiny's turn – to get a carrot for Donkey – but he couldn't resist giving Tilly a little prod to see if she really was asleep.

"Tilly," he whispered, "are you asleep?"

Tilly pretended not to hear, but opened her eyes to
see who it was and Tiny saw that she was only
pretending.

"Tilly's not sleeping, she's peeping," Tiny shouted
to Tom as he drew the curtains.

"You mean she's been pretending all the time," said
Tom as he came running into the house.

Tilly tried to tickle Tiny, and Tom joined in. He picked up the pillow and swung it this way and that. Feathers flew in all directions and the Tots collapsed in a heap, giggling and laughing.

Later, the Tots were tired. It was time for bed. As they went upstairs they heard Donkey "Ee-aw" goodnight from outside.

When they were curled up in their beds they sang – very softly – their Goodnight Song –

We've had some adventures,
some songs and some fun,
It's time now for sleeping,
our busy day's done.
So, it's Bonne Nuit, Tilly,
and Sleep Well, Tom,
It's Goodnight Tiny
– and everyone.

and very soon, all was quiet in the secret house where the Tots lived. And then from somewhere in the rafters, Furryboo gave a little "Peek a boo."